Ley Lines

Volume One

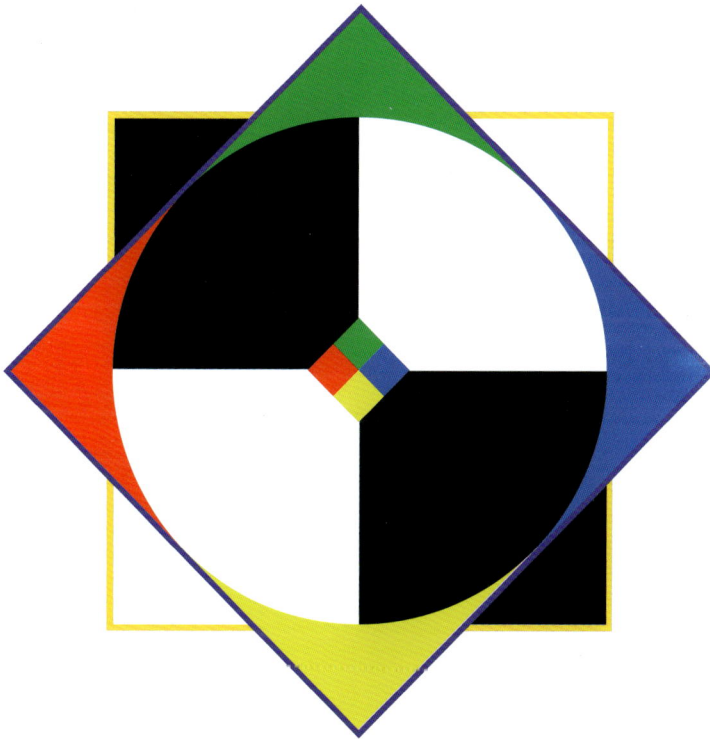

Art and Story by Robin Dempsey

www.LeyLinesComic.com

LeyLines
Volume One

Author & Artist
Robin Dempsey

Editor
Cory Childs

Assistant Colorists
J. Embleton and S. Ironmonger

© 2011, 2012 Robin Dempsey
LeyLines © and ™ Robin Dempsey
LeyLines: Volume 1 (English Edition) © MOKO Press™

M●K●
PRESS

Moko Press
Website: mokopress.com
Email: mokopress@gmail.com

ISBN # 978-0-9851253-0-1

First English printing: February 2012

Printed in China
through Active Media Printing

Dedicated to my amazing
Leylians

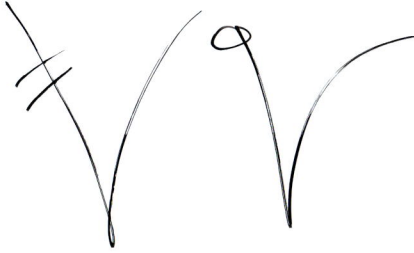

NAMA

(HONORED)

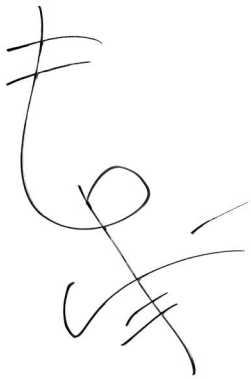

VONE

(THANKS)

to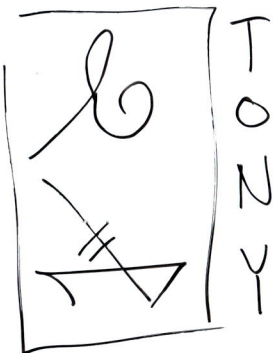

from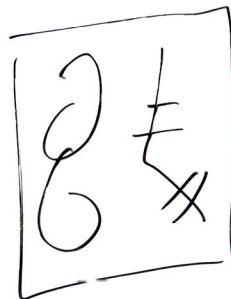

Thank you for supporting my storytelling adventure!

FIVE DAYS AGO, MY WIFE, NAIOME, WAS FOUND AT THE BOTTOM OF THE CLIFFS.
SUICIDE.
HAVE YOU SUMMONED ME HERE TO TELL ME THINGS I ALREADY KNOW, KORUVAL?
MY TIME IN THIS VESSEL IS BRIEF.
ASK YOUR QUESTIONS.

WAS THERE FOUL PLAY?
THERE IS MUCH IN YOUR CITY THAT IS FOUL.
NAIOME WAS TOUCHED BY IT AT THE TIME OF HER DEATH.
WHO MURDERED HER?
THE PAST...
...AND THE PRESENT.
ARE MY CHILDREN IN DANGER?
YOUR CHILDREN HAVE ALWAYS BEEN IN DANGER, HIGH SAGE.

VISION CURSE YOUR RIDDLES, DREAMEATER!
HE ALREADY HAS.
ANYTHING ELSE, KORUVAL OF THE VA NAZA BLOODLINE?
SOME LONG UNANSWERED QUESTION, PERHAPS?
AN UNSOLVED MYSTERY THAT HAUNTS YOUR CLAN?
WHO KILLED MY BROTHER?

YES, MY LORD.
MY APOLOGIES FOR THE MESS.
I'LL CLEAN IT UP.
DID YOU GET THE ANSWERS YOU WERE LOOKING FOR?
DON'T YOU KNOW?
WHEN THE DARK ONE GIVES, HE ALSO TAKES.
MY MEMORY HAS A NEW HOLE IN IT, I'M AFRAID.
WELL, FOR A GOD OF KNOWLEDGE, HE HAD FEW STRAIGHT ANSWERS.
I'M SORRY, MY LORD. DREAMEATER CAN BE...UNPREDICTABLE.
IT'S NOT YOUR FAULT.
THAT'S WHAT I GET FOR RELYING ON A *TIMU* GOD.
CLICK
...YES, MY LORD.

...SHE WAS THE CLOSEST I EVER HAD TO A MOTHER, SIR.
...I'M SORRY.
huh?
IT'S VERY LATE.
GET SOME REST.
THE PLAN FOR INDULGENCE DAY STILL STANDS.
YES, MY LORD.

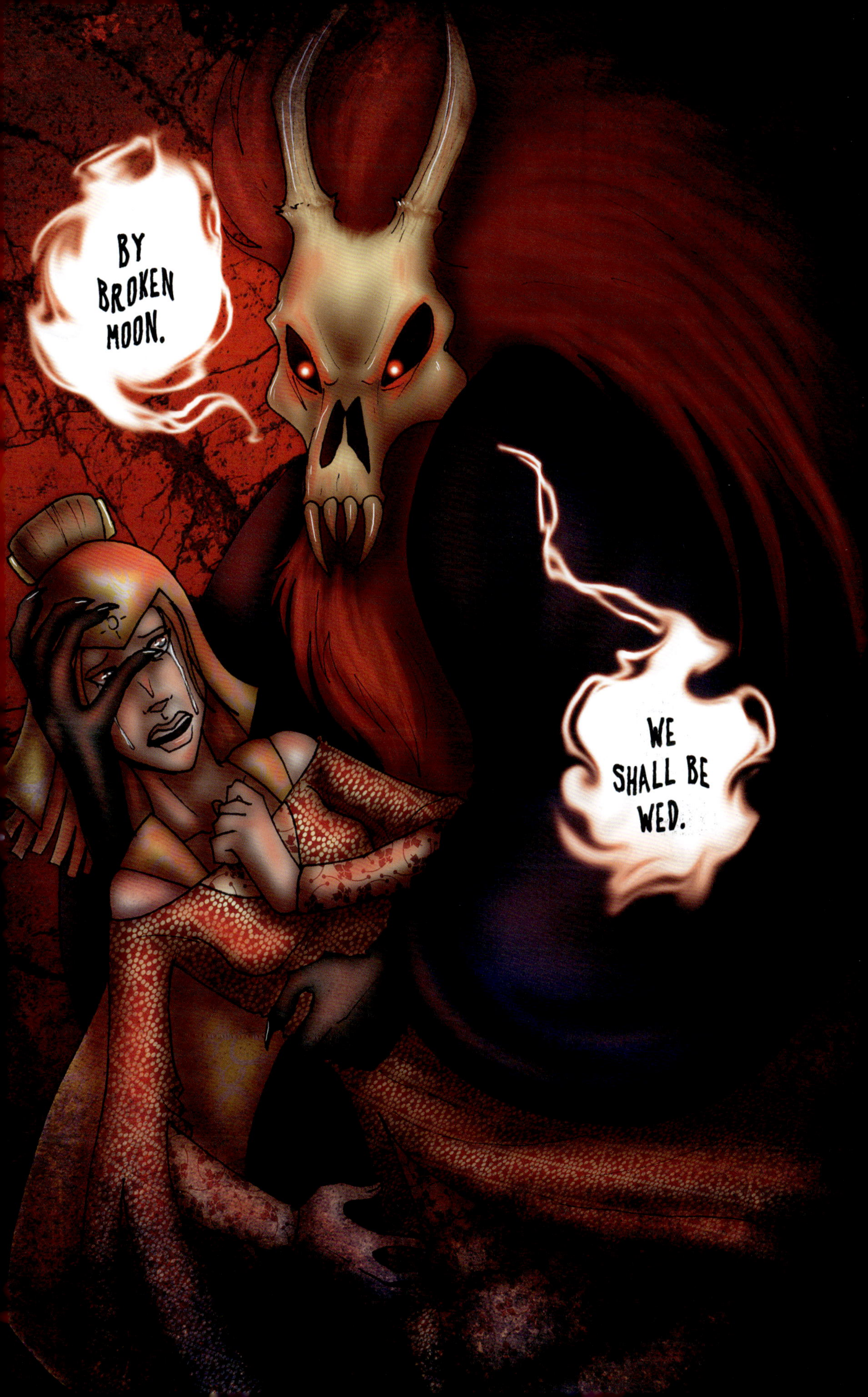
BY BROKEN MOON.
WE SHALL BE WED.

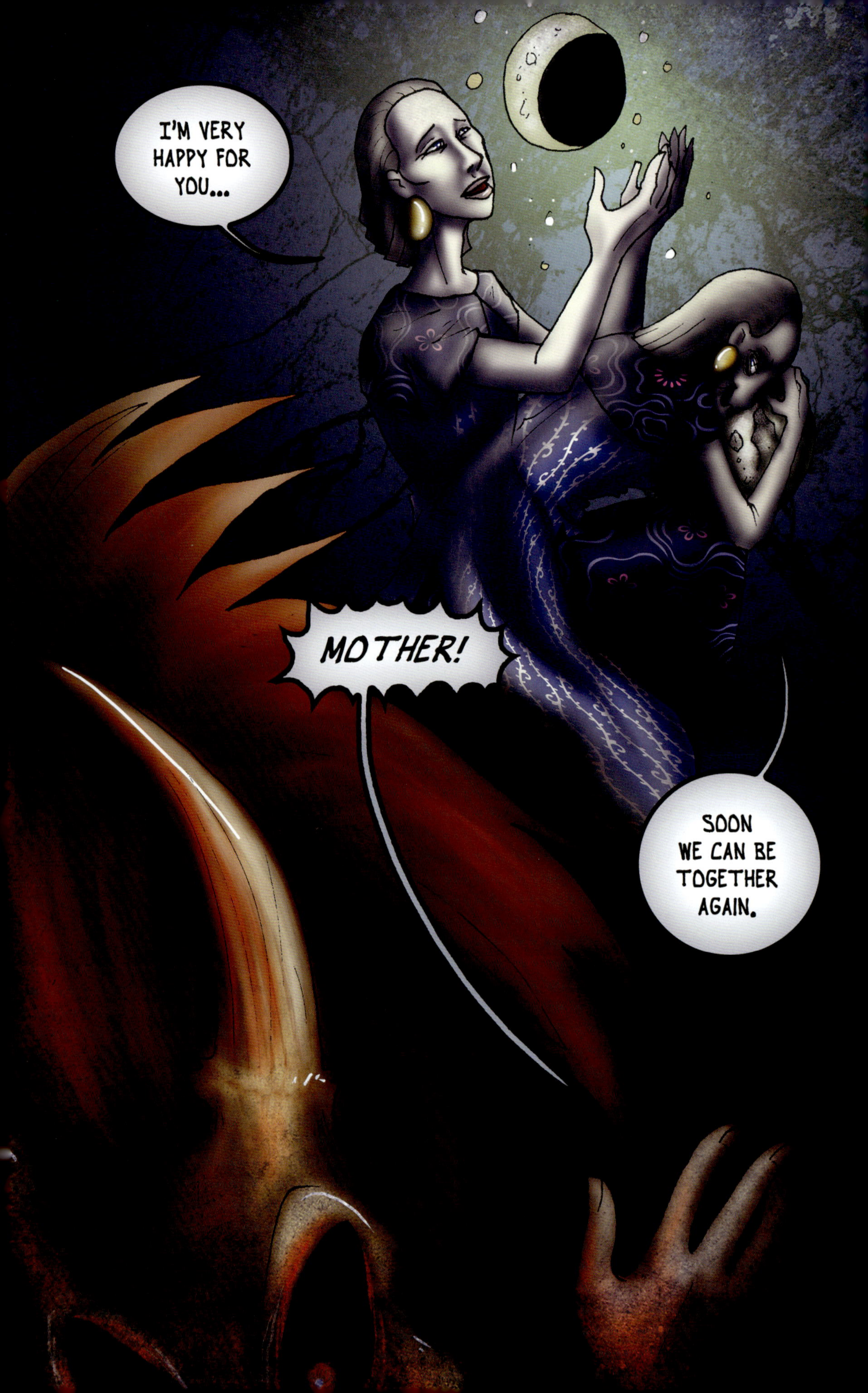
I'M VERY HAPPY FOR YOU...
MOTHER!
SOON WE CAN BE TOGETHER AGAIN.

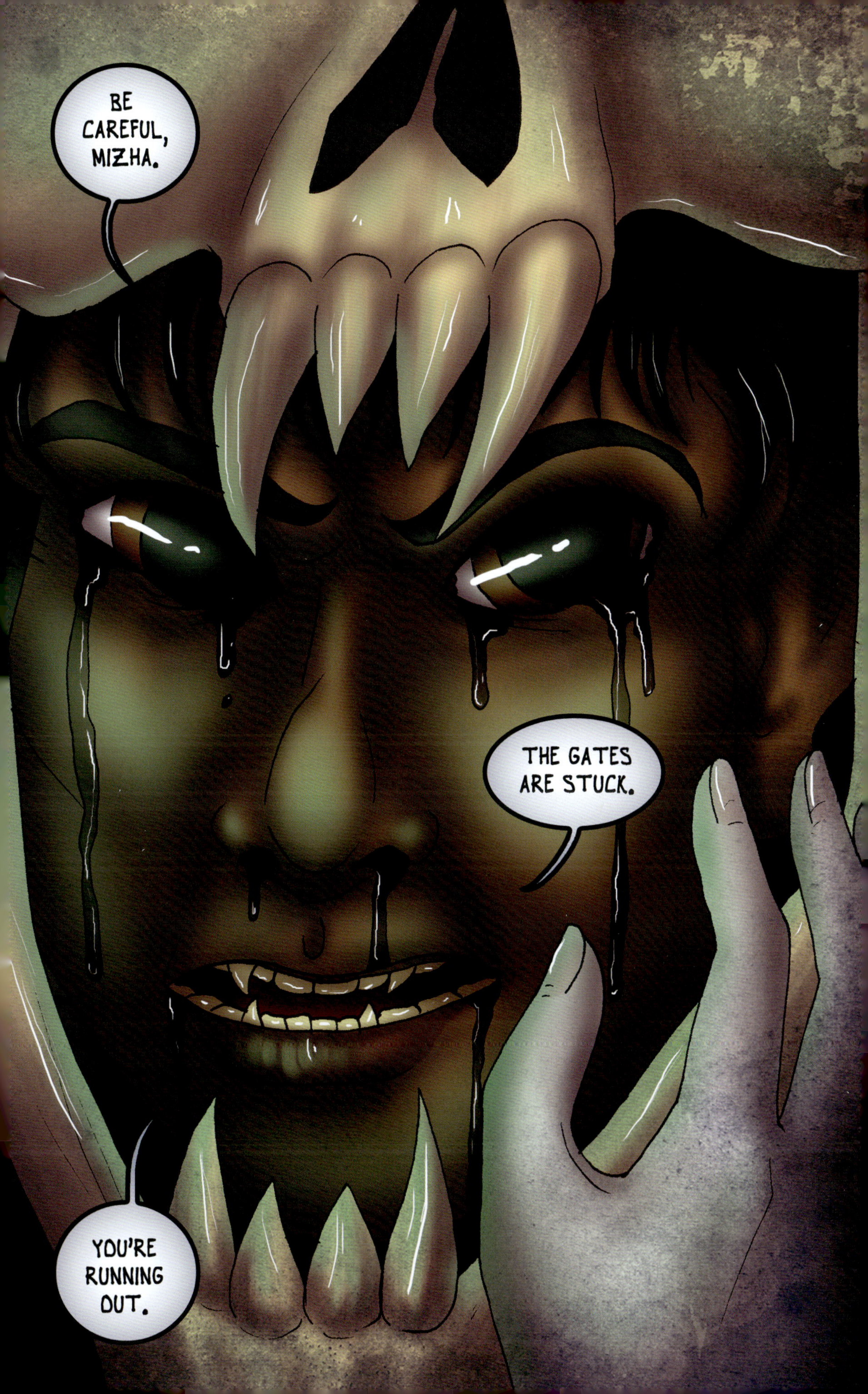
BE CAREFUL, MIZHA.
THE GATES ARE STUCK.
YOU'RE RUNNING OUT.

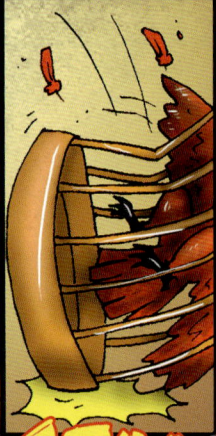

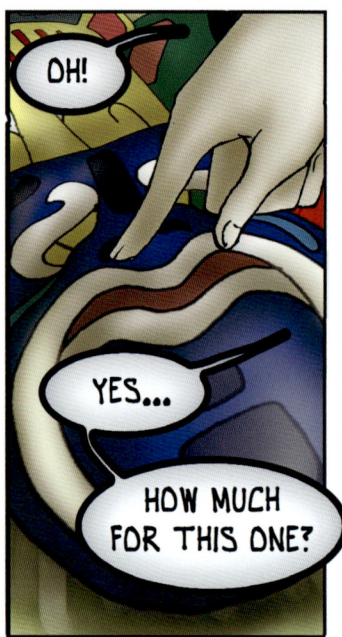

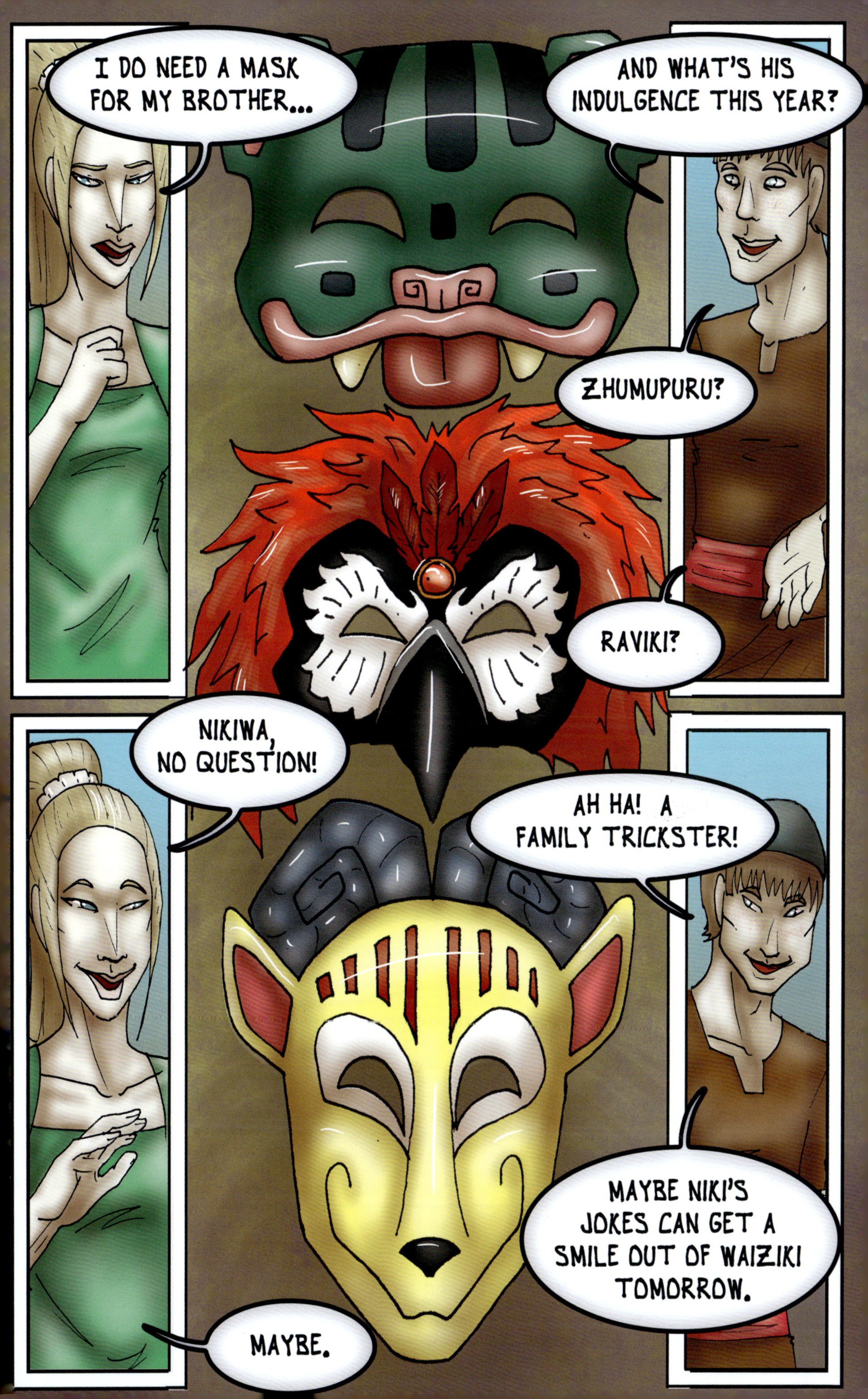
I DO NEED A MASK FOR MY BROTHER...
AND WHAT'S HIS INDULGENCE THIS YEAR?
ZHUMUPURU?
RAVIKI?
NIKIWA, NO QUESTION!
AH HA! A FAMILY TRICKSTER!
MAYBE NIKI'S JOKES CAN GET A SMILE OUT OF WAIZIKI TOMORROW.
MAYBE.

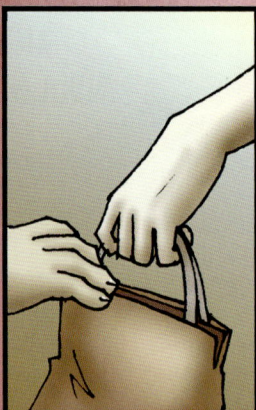

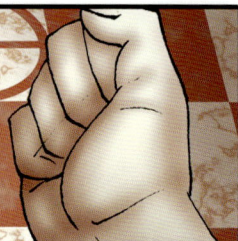

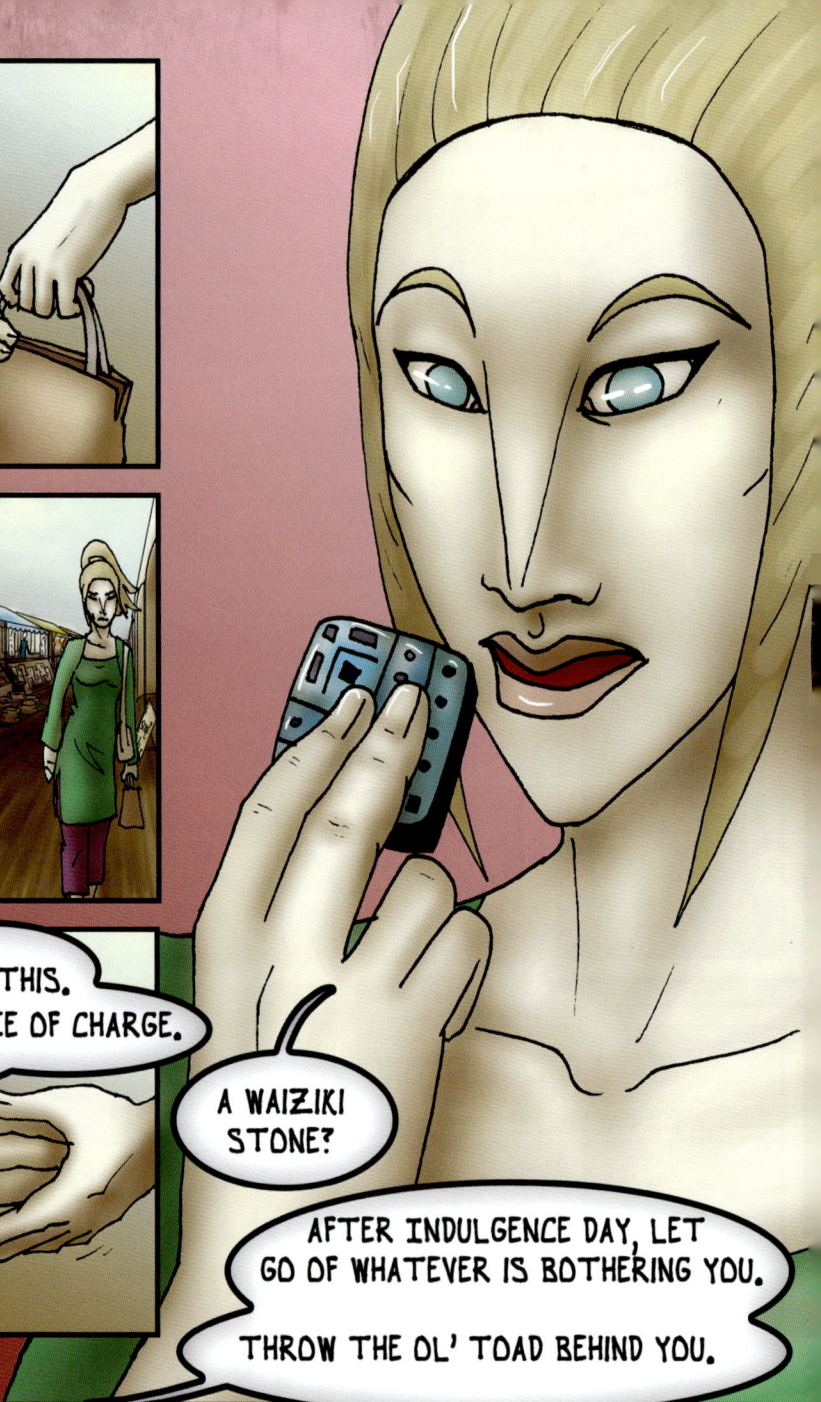

I KNOW, MIZAH.
I KNOW.
THERE'S SOMETHING I NEED TO TELL YOU.
IT'S GOING TO MEAN SOME BIG CHANGES...
FOR YOU *AND* YOUR BROTHER.
CHKA-TAK-K-CHKA-TAK-K-CHKA-TAK-K-CHKA-TAK-K-CHKA-T

HIGH SAGE, WE HAVE A PROBLEM.

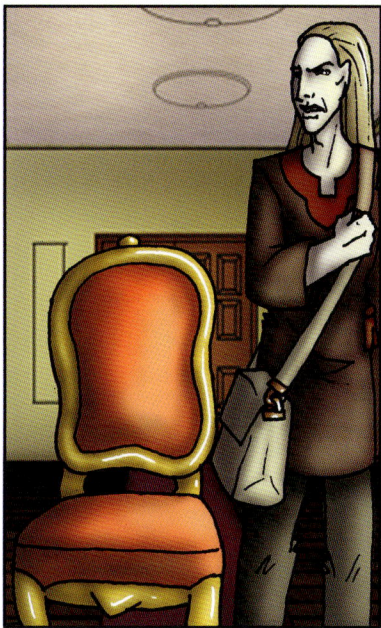

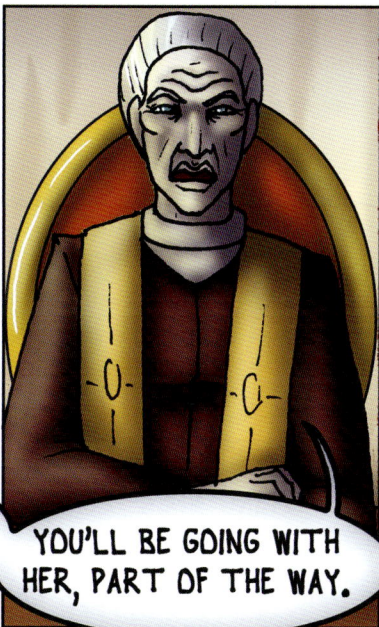

SINCE YOU'RE OBVIOUSLY NOT USING THE EDUCATION I'M PAYING FOR --
BUT I'M LEARNING!
LEARNING WHAT, EXACTLY?
CARPENTRY!
AND --
AND BAKING!
AND SEWING,
AND TANNING,
AND GRAVE DIGGING --
GRAVE DIGGING??
FATHER, HOW CAN I BE EXPECTED TO LEAD A WHOLE COUNTRY WHEN I DON'T EVEN KNOW THEIR TROUBLES?

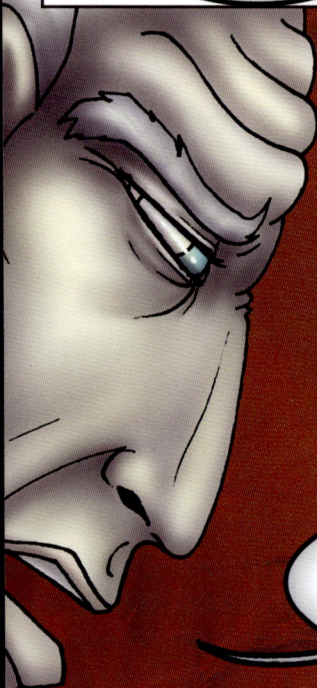

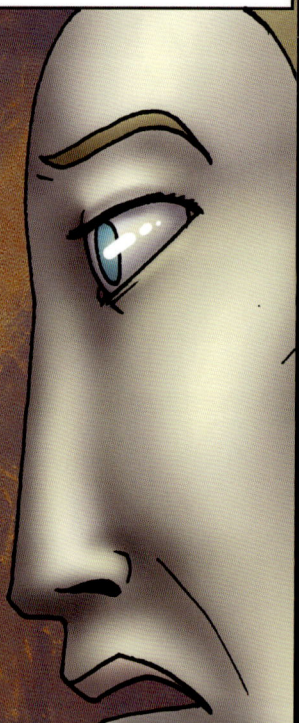

WHAT UTTER KIZAK.
YOU'RE UPROOTING OUR LIVES FOR YOUR ZHAKEN PARANOIA!!
THIS ISN'T PARANOIA!
YOUR MOTHER WAS MURDERED --!
NO! SHE WASN'T!

...YOU WILL BE LEAVING WITH MIZHA ON THE TRAIN TOMORROW, AND THAT IS FINAL.

YOU ARE DISMISSED, TAMA.

HE WILL LEAD US TO RUIN.

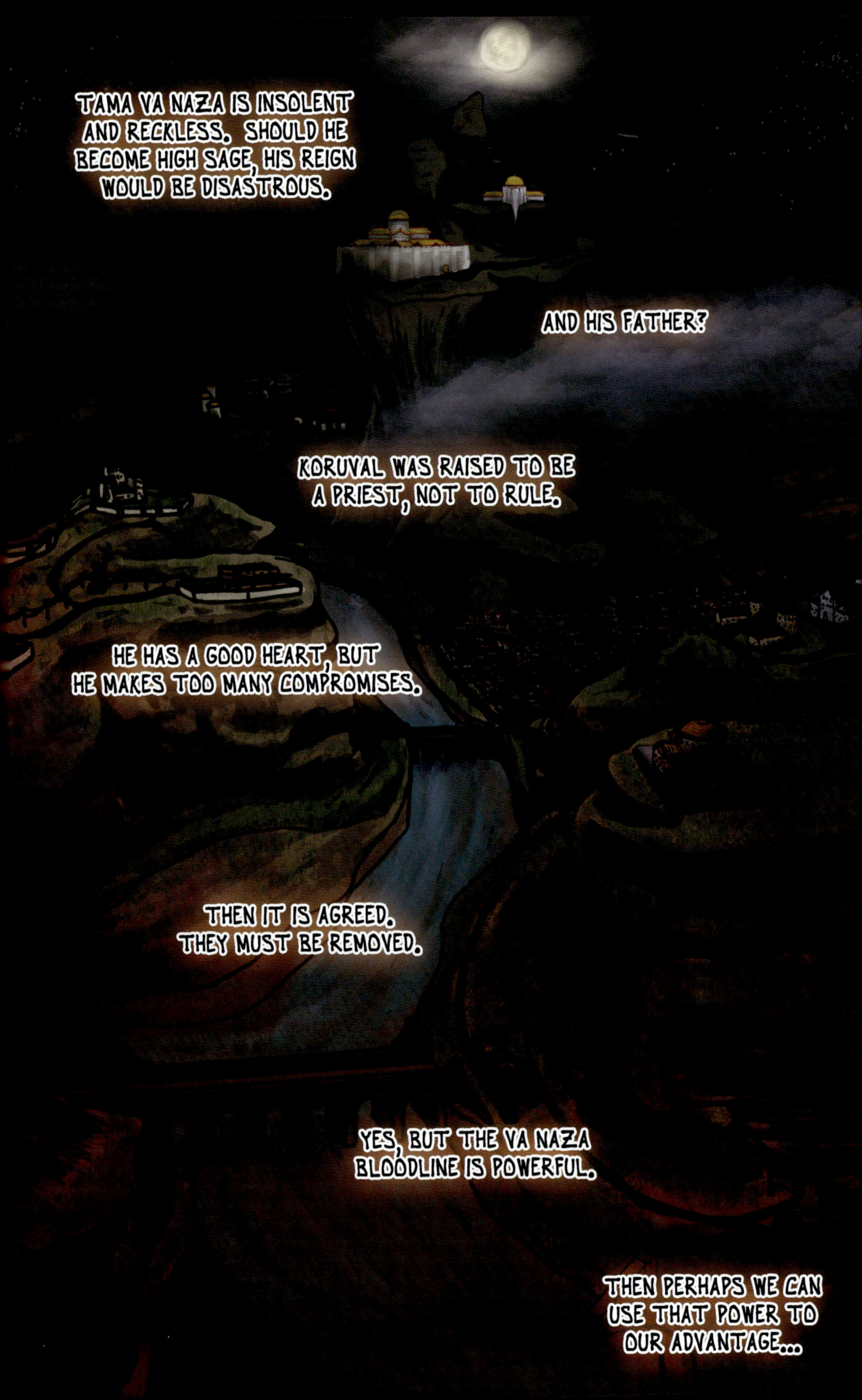

TAMA VA NAZA IS INSOLENT
AND RECKLESS. SHOULD HE
BECOME HIGH SAGE, HIS REIGN
WOULD BE DISASTROUS.

AND HIS FATHER?

KORUVAL WAS RAISED TO BE
A PRIEST, NOT TO RULE.

HE HAS A GOOD HEART, BUT
HE MAKES TOO MANY COMPROMISES.

THEN IT IS AGREED.
THEY MUST BE REMOVED.

YES, BUT THE VA NAZA
BLOODLINE IS POWERFUL.

THEN PERHAPS WE CAN
USE THAT POWER TO
OUR ADVANTAGE...

END OF CHAPTER ONE
"EVERYTHING IS FINE"

AS FOR ME...
I WAS A BULLY.
NO, YOU WERE NICE...
MIZHA, YOU CAN'T REWRITE THE PAST.
BUT MAMA SAYS IT'S THE RAINBOW GODDESS' GIFT...
MOTHER IS DEAD.
SHE GOT LOST IN HER ILLUSIONS AND SHE NEVER CAME BACK!

DON'T DO THIS TO ME, MIZHA.
I CAN'T LOSE MY MOTHER AND MY SISTER IN THE SAME WEEK.
I JUST CAN'T.

YOU'RE FINALLY BACK!
I HAVEN'T SEEN YOU IN AGES!
Oof!
MIZHA-
AND LOOK AT YOU - WHERE DID YOU FIND THESE CLOTHES?
A TRASH HEAP?
MIZHA-
AND YOUR *HAIR!*
IT'S SO LONG!
CAN I BRUSH IT?
PULU? PULU?
MIZHA!

I HEARD FATHER'S SENDING YOU TO PWAMA.
I'LL BE GOING WITH YOU. AT LEAST AS FAR AS MOMURU.
REALLY?
YEAH. WE CAN VISIT ZHIRO TOGETHER.
AT THAT CREEPY TEMPLE?
DO YOU THINK IT'S CHANGED HIM?
DID KIZHIMO CHANGE ME?
NOTHING BUT YOUR HAIR.
EXACTLY.

I BET HE HASN'T CHANGED A BIT.
IT'S DISGRACEFUL.
I BEG YOUR PARDON, CAPTAIN?
A TIMU WRITING.
IN *PUBLIC*, NO LESS!

YOU FORGOT TO DOT YOUR *ZHI*.
SMACK
AH, SO I DID.
HOW KIND OF YOU TO POINT IT OUT.
IS THAT -??
IT IS!!
ZHIRO!

BUT I SWEAR TO *ZHON*, YOU CALL ME "LORD" AGAIN AND I WILL TOSS YOU OFF A TRAIN.
FOR A MOMENT, I THOUGHT YOU'D ACQUIRED A SENSE OF PROPRIETY.
ME? THAT *WOULD* BE TRAGIC.
OH, COME ON, MIZHA. STOP SULKING AND GET OVER HERE.
OOF!
WUMPH

WHY DO YOU HAVE A TATTOO OF YOUR NAME?
IT'S A REMINDER.
"POWER BORN OF KNOWLEDGE FEEDS UPON THE MIND."
AHEM.
MY LORD AND LADY, THE TRAIN DEPARTS SOON.
WE REALLY MUST GET TO THE STATION.

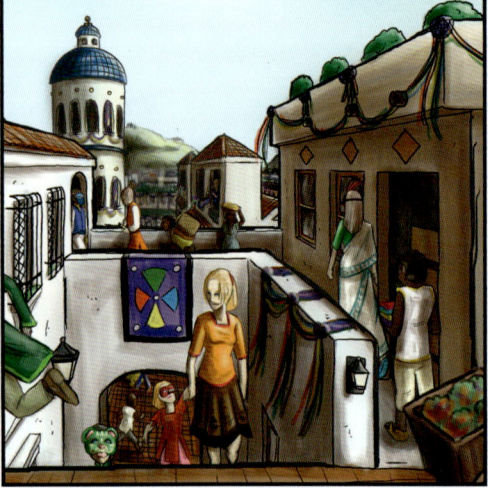

THE GUILD'S AUDITING TEAM IN KUZOPA HAS RUN INTO A SPOT OF TROUBLE.
OH?
WE HEARD FROM THE SCRIBE THREE DAYS AGO.
HIS APPRAISER HAD DISAPPEARED.
AFTER TWO DAYS OF REGULAR TELEGRAMS, WE LOST CONTACT WITH THE SCRIBE AS WELL.
THE DETAILS ARE HERE.
K-PLATCH

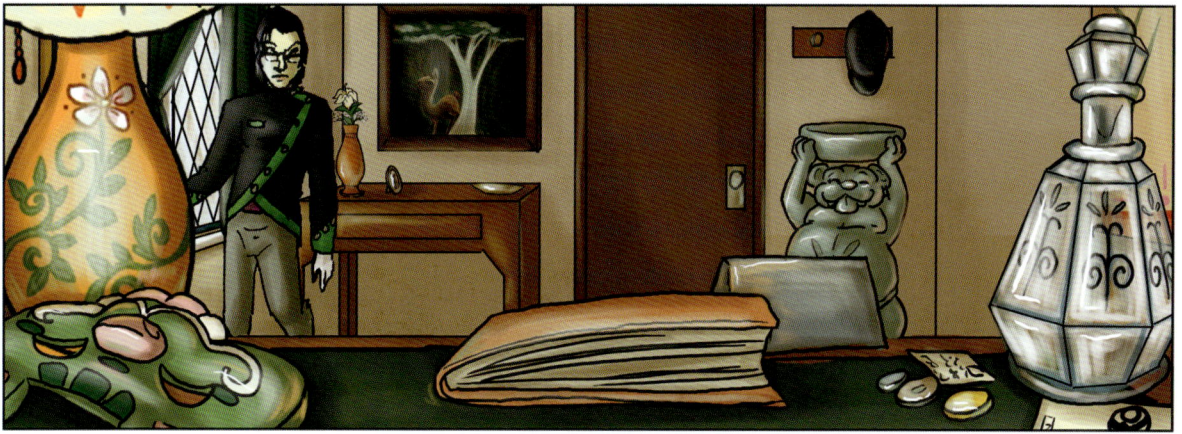

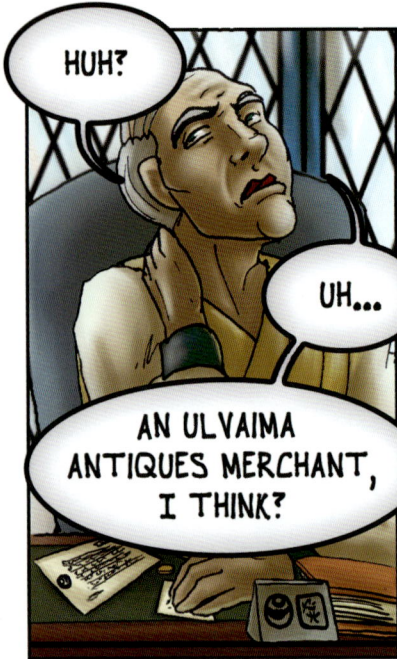

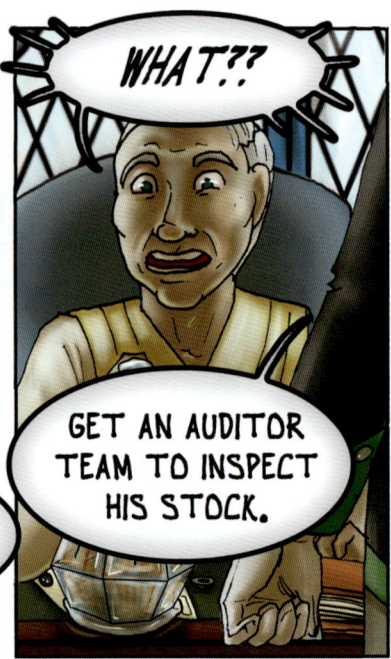

TAMAPA'O CENTRAL STATION

RELATIONSHIP:

UNKNOWN.

MIZHA?
WHAT'S WR-
OH.
I DIDN'T KNOW MOTHER'S FUNERAL CAR WOULD BE A PART OF OUR TRAIN.
HEEEYYYYY!
SO...
IS THAT WHO I THINK IT IS?

DO TRY NOT TO FALL ASLEEP AT YOUR POST, LITTLE BROTHER.
WITH YOU ABOARD?
DON'T WORRY.
I WON'T.
END CHAPTER TWO "MASKED INTENTIONS"

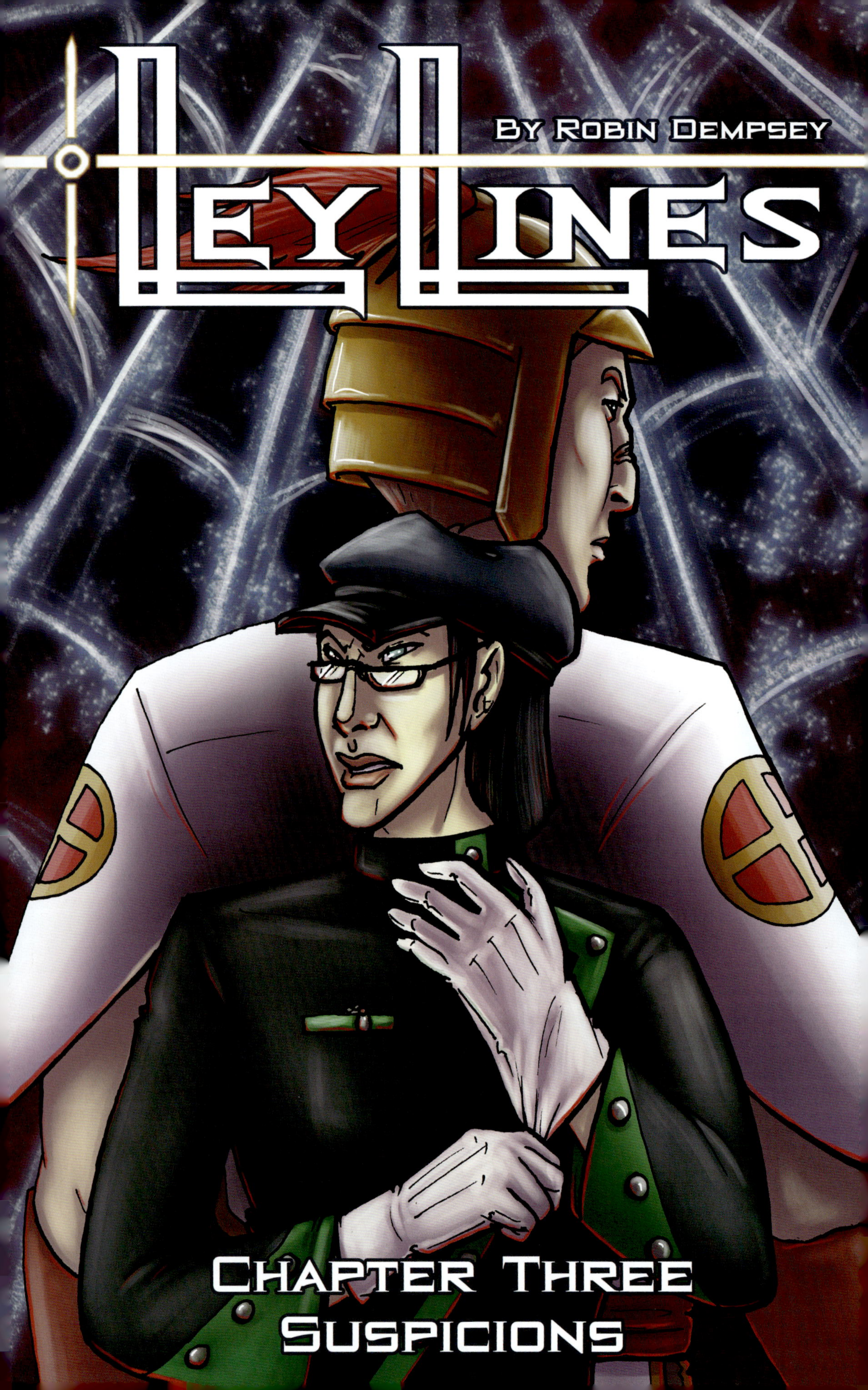
By Robin Dempsey
Ley Lines
Chapter Three
Suspicions

THIS ISN'T LIKE YOU, KOA.
CRASHING INTO ME AT THE STATION?
RISKY.
I HAD TO BE SURE I COULD TALK TO YOU BEFORE REACHING MOMURU.
WHAT'S WRONG?
MY SOURCES TELL ME YOUR BROTHER, NOREN, IS KEEPING SOME *UNUSUAL* COMPANY.
PIRATES, YOU MEAN.

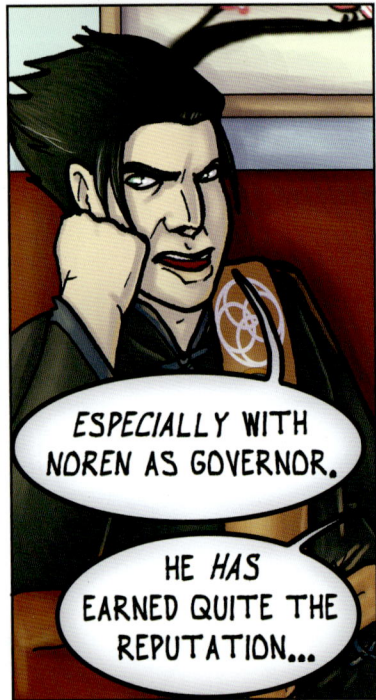

IS EVERYTHING ALL RIGHT MY LORD?
NO! EVERYTHING IS *NOT* ALL RIGHT! MY SISTER IS A RUTHLESS, *CHEATING* CARD-PLAYER!
I DO *NOT* CHEAT!
YOU JUST DON'T UNDERSTAND STRATEGY.
STRATEGY?
THEN WHY AREN'T YOU JUST AS EVIL TO ZHIRO? IS *THAT* PART OF YOUR STRATEGY?
OBVIOUSLY BECAUSE HE'S CUTER THAN YOU, BIG BROTHER.
sigh
NOW QUIT STALLING AND DISCARD YOUR CARDS, YOU BIG BABY.

SOMETHING IS WRONG ON THIS TRAIN...NAMELY, ITS PASSENGERS.

ROUGH. CHEAP COTTON, VILAZOSHU.

LAVENDER, OIL HARVESTED IN ULVAIMA.

SQUEEK, FLUTE NOT CORRECTLY CARVED.

RASPING VOICE, AZHIZ SMOKER

URINE, WOAD DYER? HOPEFULLY.

SWEET LIME, TANNER

RATTLE, LOOSE SCREW ON LUGGAGE RACK

WHISTLE, WINDOW NOT PROPERLY SHUT

ACRID SMOKE - CHEAP AZHIZ

INK, SCRIBE.

CREAK, DOOR HINGE REQUIRES OILING

SIR?

LURCHING. POSSIBLE WHEEL WEAR ON LEFT SIDE OF CAR - SPEAK TO CONDUCTOR?

SOAP? SOMEONE WHO ACTUALLY BATHES IS HERE?

SIR?

HEAT. APPROXIMATELY 100 PEOPLE IN CAR? CAN'T BREATHE.

INCENSE - A PAGAN'S HERE?

EXCUSE ME, SIR, ARE YOU ALL RIGHT?

NOT FEELING WELL.

PLEASE?

SWITCH PLACES?

TRADITIONAL ULVAIMA GARB. TYPICALLY ONLY WORN BY DESCENDANTS OF THE ORIGINAL TRIBE.
BLACK HAIR. INDICATES PWAMA ANCESTRY.
SILK. KIZHIMO. RARE, FAR TOO EXPENSIVE FOR COMMON MERCHANT.
ZHUMUWELO BUTTON DESIGN. RARELY SEEN OUTSIDE PROVINCE.
MOMURU BLACKSMITH GUILD INSIGNIA, BUT NO SCENT OF FORGE MATERIALS, WRONG BUILD, NO EVIDENCE OF WORKING CALLUSES.
WELL?
UH...
NO, SIR.
THERE IS NOTHING WRONG WITH YOUR FACE.

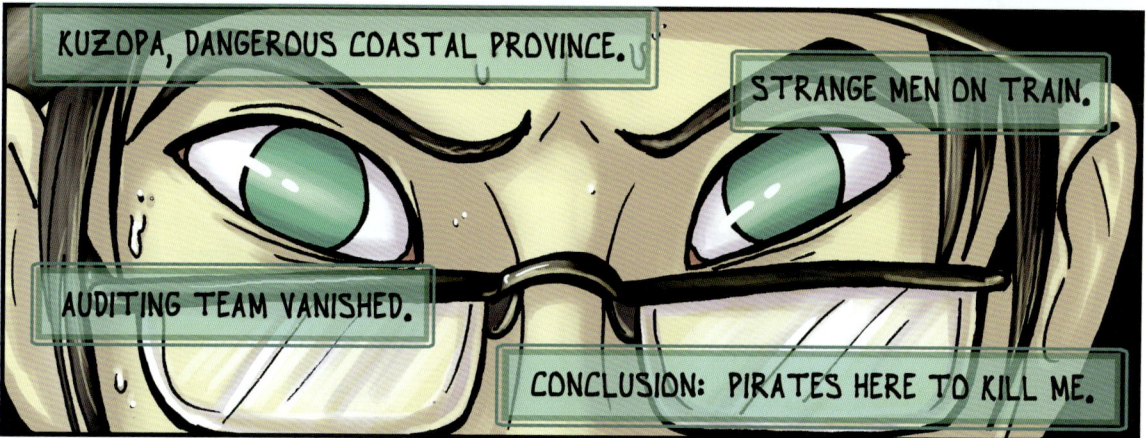

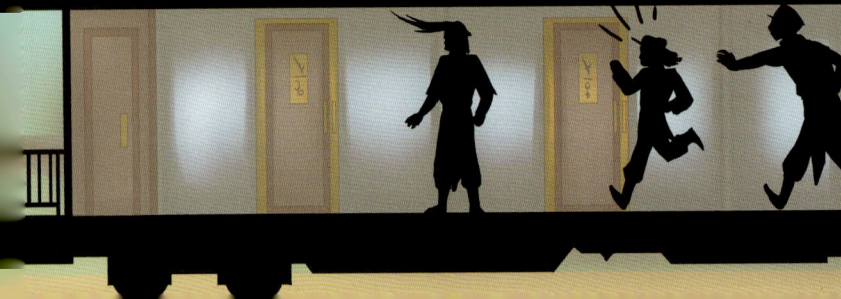

I AM GUILD MASTER AUDITOR PAKKU.
YOU'VE BLOWN YOUR COVER.
START IT NOW.
...AND THERE ARE PIRATES ON THIS TRAIN.

...TO NEW FRIENDS IN TROUBLED TIMES.
GUARDS!
THERE ARE ROBBERS ON THE TRAIN!
WHAT? HOW MANY?
AT LEAST A DOZEN TWO CARS DOWN!
AND I HEARD ONE SAY THAT THE TIMU WERE GOING TO TAKE CARE OF THE ENGINE!
KIZAK!
MAILO AND I WILL GO TELLTHE CAPTAIN.
THE REST OF YOU, STOP THOSE ROBBERS!
YES SIR!

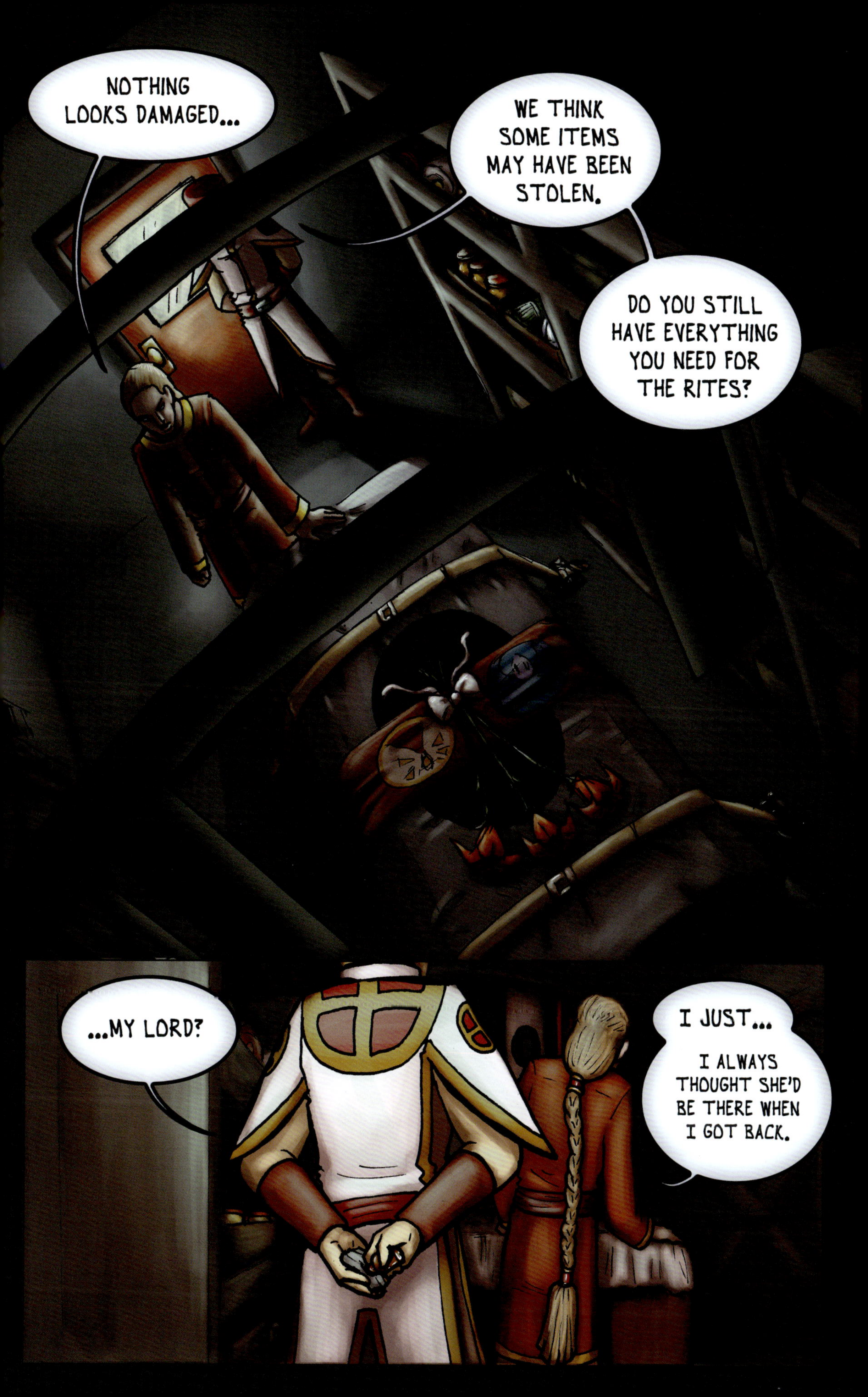
NOTHING LOOKS DAMAGED...
WE THINK SOME ITEMS MAY HAVE BEEN STOLEN.
DO YOU STILL HAVE EVERYTHING YOU NEED FOR THE RITES?
...MY LORD?
I JUST...
I ALWAYS THOUGHT SHE'D BE THERE WHEN I GOT BACK.

SHE WAS MY MOTHER.
I NEVER GOT TO SAY GOOD-BYE.
YOU HAD MORE TIME WITH HER THAN SOME.
YOU SHOULD HONOR HER MEMORY BY BEING STRONG.
RIGHT.
HOW COULD I *FORGET?*
SHOW NO WEAKNESS.
HAVE NO *SOUL.*
IT'S THE ITSURI WAY.

SMILE, TAMA!
YOU DESCENDED FROM GOD!
MAKE SURE THERE'S HONEY AT THE FUNERAL.
THIS IS A CELEBRATION, AFTER ALL.
HAVE TO HONOR THE GREAT VISION!
NEVER MIND THAT HE TOOK YOUR MOTHER!
NEVER MIND THAT -
ENOUGH!

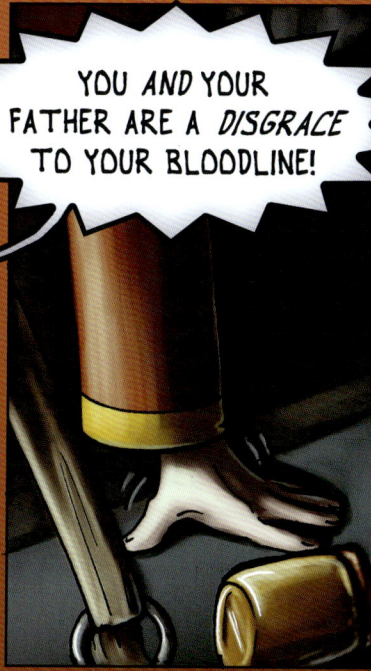

SMACK

THUD

FATHER WAS RIGHT...

STAY BACK!!

SOMEONE IS TRYING TO KILL US:

OUR OWN GUARDS!

CRACK

TAKE MY HAND.
MIZHA? GET OUT OF HERE! RUN!
PROMISE ME, YOU WON'T LET GO.
WHAT?
PROMISE!
WHAK
Augh!
...
I PROMISE.

MIZHA VA NAZA AND I SHALL BE WED.

END CHAPTER THREE
"SUSPICIONS"

EXTRAS

The land of the *Tamakepe* and *Timu* is vast, containing a wide variety of cultures, traditions, and local histories. I've put together veritable tomes of information for this tale in the form of sketches, maps, and explanations. The best of these will be included in the printed volumes, for those that love the little details as much as I do.

The first extra is a 21-page story that was created on October 1st, 2011, during the annual 24-Hour Comic Day. For those of you not familiar with the tradition, the challenge was first posed by Scott McCloud, to create 24 pages of comic material in 24 hours. It has become a world-wind event, and I spent mine at Time Warp Comics in Boulder, Colorado, one of the finest comic stores I've ever had the pleasure to peruse. It was the first time I had ever attempted the task, so I planned for a "modest" 21 page creation instead of the full 24. I finished about 7 hours early and passed out under a table after going just a tad bit insane. So next year I'm aiming for 24 pages, possibly in color, just to drive myself 100% crazy instead of 70.83% bonkers like last year.

So, without further delay I present to you, complete with commentary...

RYARO and the TAIL of FIRE
by Robin Dempsey
leylinescomic.com

SAGE BUNAI HAS ASKED US TO DISCUSS THIS PASSAGE. QUESTIONS?

THIS IS *BORING*.

CAN'T YOU TELL US A STORY?

A STORY?

WELL...

ALL RIGHT.

JUST DON'T TELL THE SAGE!

The current religion is not the original form of worship in the *LeyLines* world. Although the followers of Vision have existed for centuries, wide-spread Visionary religious domination did not start until roughly fifty to sixty years ago. The *Itsuri* conquerers had run into a bit of trouble in their efforts to unite the world's peoples under the High Sage's rule. Namely, *Pwama's* Great Wall. As the *Itsuri* expansion stagnated in decades of gaining and losing the same bits of ground, the Sun Sages, religious advisors to the High Sage, turned their attention to homogenizing the land they already controlled, including the systematic degradation and absorption of existing "pagan" traditions. This tale takes place during the first attempts to "civilize" the "barbaric Timu" of the South and West.

Originally there were eight gods, worshipped universally, but with different emphasis in different areas, where one god in particular might be seen as a Patron. Rakaro's Wife would later be known as the *Tamakepe* Rainbow Goddess, while Rakaro became the frightening *Timu* god Dream Eater.

On the top page you can just make out the giant ram, the original form of *Nikiwa*, guardian of the Spirits of the Dead and Master of the Four Winds. Having the wind in one's favor was seen as a gift from *Nikiwa*, and even today he is worshipped by superstitious sailors as a god of good fortune.

The name "Night Spider" is still used to describe The Bone Matron, dark oracle of prophecy. Even in her original form, she was a bit of a nasty character, vain, patronizing, and convinced of her own wisdom. It's easy to think you're smarter than everyone else when you can see the future.

Rakaro's personality is heavily influenced by Anansi. They were some of my favorite tales as a child, although my imagining changed to include aspects of Neil Gaiman's version in *Anansi Boys*. As in many of those stories, the biggest joke is that anybody trusts him enough to be fooled.

The Great Green Bear *Zhumupuru* once represented generosity and compassion. He was guardian of the newly dead, responsible for returning bodies to the earth and shepherding souls to *Nikiwa* in the Canyon of Whispers. Although Visionaries have attempted to warp him into the manifestation of lust, sloth, and greed, many rural communities still worship his original form.

BUT HIS WIFE SAW ONLY THE RED OF HIS TAIL, AND DESPAIRED. "ALL THE WATER IS GONE, BUT YOU STILL BURN! HUSBAND, I CANNOT BEAR IT! I WILL FIND HELP!" AND SO SHE FLEW...

I AM SORRY, DREAMER, BUT I HAVE GIVEN ALL. THE MORNING DEW IS LOST.

I AM SORRY, DREAMER, BUT I HAVE NOTHING TO GIVE AND THE GREAT FORREST IS NOW DYING.

CAN NONE HELP MY POOR HUSBAND?

HAS OUR WORLD COME TO RUIN?

WE ARE SORRY, DREAMER, WE HAVE DONE ALL WE CAN.

AND TORN THE EARTH IN OUR HASTE.

WELL, *THIS* DOESN'T SOUND LIKE YOUR VISIONARY PASSAGE!

"Dreamer" is another name for the Rainbow Goddess still used in *Pwama* culture today. Unlike the people of *Itsuri*, the *Pwama* worship Dreamer as their highest deity, not the "upstart, barbaric Vision" of their historic enemies. Current belief is that Vision is brother to Dreamer, but whether he is the elder, younger, twin, friend, enemy, ally or usurper depends on who you ask.

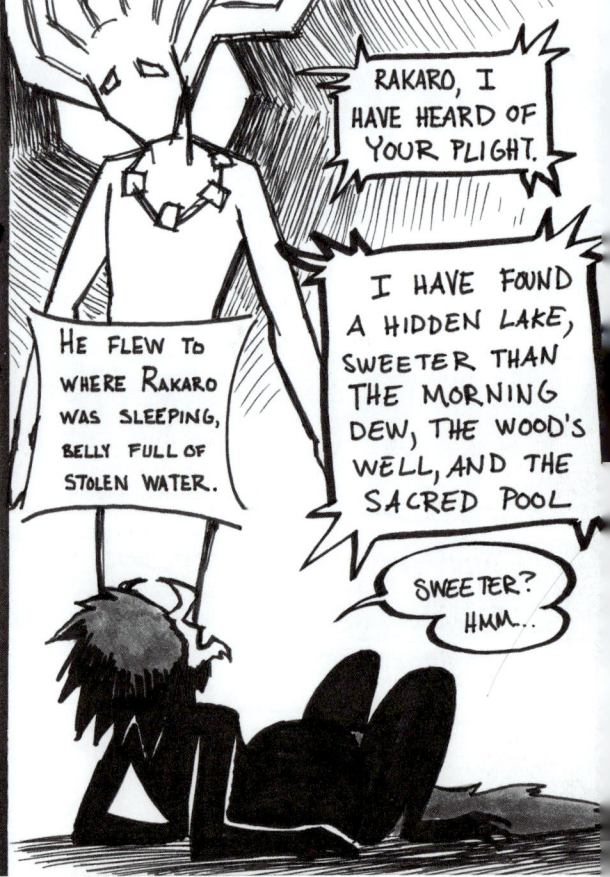

Poor Ravazhi. He has no idea how one of his favorite folk tales is about to change forever. This is where Rakaro's portrayal began to get altered from a trickster to a villain. I decided to change the artwork slightly as well, depicting Vision as a being of pure light and Rakaro as pure darkness.

Vision is not a kind god. His primary Virtues are ambition, strength, and loyalty. Forgiveness, kindness, and patience, while not exactly considered bad traits, are still viewed as weaknesses of character if they are allowed to conflict with the primary Virtues.

This is not all that far from how the original story ends. Rakaro is the Patron god of the volcano near Momuru, and this tale is to explain, in part, how that happened. It also recorded a great drought and tribal wars between many centuries ago. Except that Vision's tribe was not the victor.

THAT'S...NOT EXACTLY HOW I'VE HEARD THE STORY TOLD...

IT'S TRUE. THERE ARE MANY ENDINGS TO THIS TALE...

SOME SAY VISION DID NOT HELP AT ALL, BUT THE EAST WITCH. OTHERS SAY IT WAS A BLUE FROG.

BUT EVERYONE KNOWS THOSE PEOPLE ARE FOOLS, RIGHT BROTHER RAVAZHI?

YES SIR. ONLY FOOLS.

VISION and the HIDDEN LAKE

OR RAKARO and the TAIL of FIRE - ～ A FOOL'S TALE ～

We will meet Ravazhi again. He later left the Visionary church, traveling the world to document the original stories and traditions of other cultures. As *Itsuri*'s first antrhopologist, he founded the archaeology program at Kizhimo's University before mysteriously vanishing 30 years ago...

ORIGINS

The original story idea I had was vastly different than what you now hold in your hands. Here's just a small sampling of what changed from my initial brainstorming.

(left) This is the first image ever created for LeyLines, and the first version of Mizha. At that time the title was *Child of Darkness.* And it was much more tragic and angsty. It was awful, but, more importantly, it got me started.

(right) One thing that hasn't changed from the original is that the va Naza family has issues. Lots of them. Mizha was originally going to sacrifice herself to a god of darkness. Convinced by her father that this was for the good of her people, she later learned it was all just a ruse for the High Sage to gain more power. Koruval was a flat, evil character. I found it very boring and unsatisfying, so I started to flesh his character out more. By the time I'd finished, he no longer made any sense as an antagonist, and the story was re-written, keeping the cast, but creating stronger stories.

None shall understand the sacrifice you make this day.

But we will remember, my daughter, how you gave yourself to darkness for your people. And for your father.

Originally the story was a post-apocalyptic science fiction. The Lightbringers were aliens that had enslaved the human race. Small bands of nomadic rebels opposed the aliens, aided by a sentient, mutant rat race that called themselves the Rtsktn.

The original version of Kali, pictured here in a wolf-mask with her Rtsktn friend, was one such Nomad, on a quest to free her sister from Lightbringer enslavement. I dropped the sister and the Rtsktn. Mostly because I discovered that I hated drawing giant rats. Kali's goggles and practical clothing stayed.

Most of the humans on this world had been turned into "Sleepers" by the Lightbringers. All their nerve endings had been systematically disconnected from their brains and re-routed to Sleeper collars, pictured on the left, which controlled all their motor functions. The collars also flooded the brain with mood-altering drugs, to keep Sleepers docile. Hence the name, as most would act as though asleep even when active.

Kali's sister was a Sleeper. This character got over-hauled many, many times. Elements of the Sleepers carried over into the slow degradation of the mind that Illusionists suffer when using their gift to excess. The late Lady va Naza is an example of this. As for the character, she eventually became Anna, a member of the cast we'll meet in a later book.

Of the original cast, Tama is the most unchanged. He's always taken the well-being of his sister and adopted brother seriously, but he gained a mischievous side as I developed him. Mizha started as a moody, brooding character, but changed into a bubbly personality with hidden strengths. Yet it is probably Zhiro that saw the most changes. Although he was always a monk, the way I first imagined him was a chipper, irresponsible book-worm that couldn't fight to save his life and got through most problems by being a fast-talker and incredibly skilled mooch.

Since then, many of those qualities were incorporated into Tama's personality, and I started Zhiro's character mostly from scratch. He also went through a variety of names, including Tobias, Tova, Terat, Teri, Zilai, and Ziro. A big turning point for the development of Zhiro was the creation of the Timu race. The science-fiction alien thing had quickly broken down when gods entered the story, and I decided that neither race would be human. The relationship between the races shaped Zhiro's history.

However, then I had to design a new race! I wanted the Timu to seem more predatory and animalistic. However, since Zhiro was a main cast member, the Timu also needed to have a design that could still appear friendly.

The image on the left is from about half-way through the design process. The image on the top-right is the final version of Timu, depending on region. Since there is a vast variety of face-shapes in humans from one continent to the next, it made sense to develop different local traits in Timu as well. Starting from the top left and going in a clock-wise direction we have Eastern, Northern, Western, and Southern Timu.

Zhiro does not know who his birth parents are, but his facial structures indicate a mix of Timu from the East and North. A perfect combination that can be either adorable or intimidating.

GODS

As you saw in the Rakaro Fool's Tale, many of the gods had drastically different forms than their modern incarnations. This is how Vision, the Rainbow Goddess, and Bone Matron are portrayed now. Vision is now considered a Sun God. The Rainbow Goddess is the Lady of a Sacred Lake near the Pwama capitol.

The Bone Matron is the goddess of prophecy, fortune-telling, and childbirth. Her form is see-through, exposing the skeletal structure underneath. Out of one empty eye socket a snake coils out of her skull, down through her ribs, and emerges at the middle of her stomach. This design is based in part on a piece of Germanic folk art I saw while visiting the Tiroler Volkskunstmuseum in Innsbruck, Austria. It was, of all things, a towel rack, in the form of a carved wooden woman. Half the figure was a lovely queen, complete with crown. The other half was a skeleton, with a snake coiling about the collar bone. I found the image fascinating in a haunting and unsettling way. The Bone Matron seemed perfect to Incorporate some of those elements.

I've gotten a lot of reader questions on how extensively the Bone Matron can interfere with the world. Just like all the other gods, she has to act through a proxy. Although it is possible for her to assume control of a vessel if they are properly trained and have the needed abilities, she typically can only send those born with her gift warnings and visions.

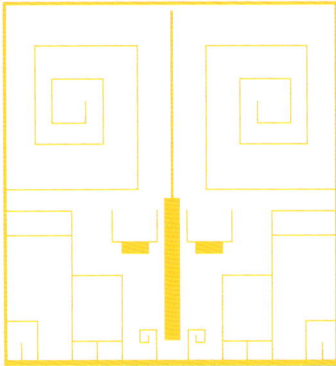

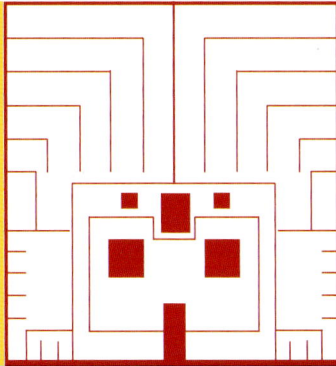

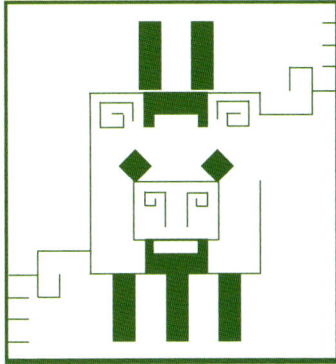

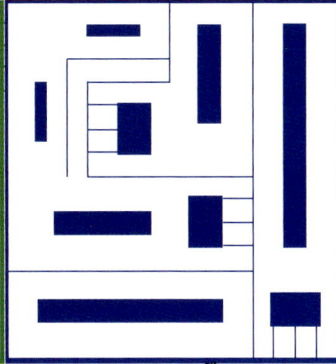

Originally each of the eight gods was associated with a sacred number and time of year in addition to location. Although each area had its Patron god, all gods were worshipped according to their season.

Nikiwa, Storm Caller, Guardian of the Canyon of Souls. Associated with the number one, Spring, & South.

Raviki, Sky Fire, God of the Sun and Guardian of the Holy Fire. Associated with the number three, Summer, & West.

Zhumupuru, Earth Shaker, Guardian of the Green Wood. Associated with the number five, Autumn, & North.

Waiziki, Rain Maker, Guardian of Wisdom. Associated with the number seven, Winter, & East.

Zhumupuru under Visionary alteration became the Indulgence of physical desire. For years, Visionaries have attempted to depict him as jealous hedonist, coveting the enjoyment of others. However, the most common and enduring version is simply a well-meaning, bumbling character that lets greed get the better of him. The Great Green Bear is still quietly worshipped in many places according to the old ways, particularly in Zhumuwelo.

Waiziki, the weeping frog, is the Indulgence of self-serving emotions. Pity, doubt, grief, mercy, vanity, shame, pride, and depression are all considered signs of Waiziki's influence. It was once believed that the rain was Waiziki's pure tears, sent to purify the earth and cleanse the mind of falsehoods. Now, her shrines are abandoned, her temple forgotten. Much like the Waiziki stone, she has been tossed over the culture's shoulder and left in the dust of the past.

Also known as the raving "Owl of Madness," Raviki is the Indulgence of passion. Love, wrath, and attachment are examples of emotions that, if allowed to rage out of control, can drive a person insane. While Visionaries do not claim that love or anger on their own are wicked, excessive expression of those feelings, particularly in public, is considered taboo. Lightbringers are expected to always remain calm and serene.

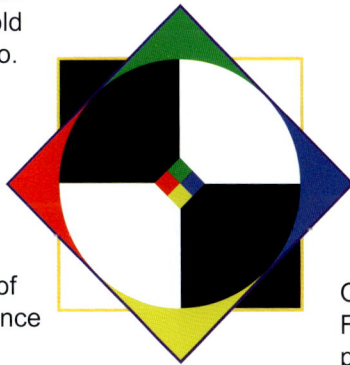

Of the Indulgences, Nikiwa the Foolish Ram is one of the most popular, particularly among children. He represents the indulgence of frivolousness. He's associated with laziness and the inability to keep commitments. Festivals at the first snow melt celebrating Spring in his honor are still common. However, rather than giving thanks to the wind, these holidays are full of pranks and mischief.

PEOPLE

Since we've already covered a lot of the Main Cast in the Origins section, I thought I'd focus on members of the Investigation Cast and Villain Cast.

Warren's design, other than giving him a more formal uniform, remains fairly unchanged from his first sketch (right). In answer to several reader questions, Warren got the massive scar and disfigured nose from Tama. Warren was raised at the palace. Since he was several years older and of a lower class than his childhood playmates, he never got along well with the Scion. Unbeknownst to Warren, Tama had just decided after a year of bullying that Zhiro was his blood-brother. Warren slighted Zhiro in some small way and Tama went over-board in trying to defend his new brother's honor. Warren, unable to truly fight back since Tama would one day be his Lord, suffered the consequences.

Pakku, originally named Palu, had the most drastic character re-design of almost any LeyLines character. In his first incarnation, (far right) he was much younger, with no special abilities or rank. A low-level scribe, he was assigned to the dubious honor of serving in the Pwama ambassador's household. Except that I also wanted him to be a anthropologist and an expert on Pwama and Itsuri cultures. This combination did not make any sense. Nor could I think of a way for him to get involved in the events on the train. The character history was thread-bare, and it showed.

Warren and Pakku (Palu)

PAKKU VA WULKA

GUILD AUDITOR

So I went back to the beginning, but not with Pakku. No, I went to the origins of the Merchant Guilds. In designing their systems of governance, I came up with the concept of Auditors and Auditing Teams. A Team is made of a Scribe and Appraiser. Once members of a team have proven their skill and integrity, they can be promoted to Auditors, capable of investigating breaches of Guild Law independently. I knew that Pakku would be such an individual, and that he would need to have unique abilities for the job.

His conflicts with his family rose in part from these unique skills, but mostly from issues I was dealing with at the time of his creation. He is my vehicle for processing those recent events. We'll be digging into his history more in future chapters. As for Vepina, since many of you were curious about her, if you've gotten this far, you've seen her once already. Check the divider page between Chapters Two and Three.

Dr. Zal va Milan
Journeyman Doctor and
Order of Eclipse Assassin

The coat ties back, but can be folded forward to create a protective layer

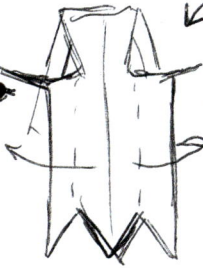

My beloved villains! Originally the entire train scene was going to have nothing but face-less, no-name bad guys. It was boring and unsatisfying. So I figured the best way to improve it was to give the antagonists identities. I enjoyed writing them so much that I decided to make them reoccurring villains!

Lu Pai was the first character that I made for the Villain Cast, but I was trying to make him too many things - rough and tumble country man *and* sophisticated tactician. I split those ideas apart and created Milan. While Lu Pai is the older of the two by about twenty years, Dr. Milan is the leader of their cell. The reason for this is that Lu Pai was enlisted in the Order. Dr. Milan is an Officer. The last member of their team is the Crimson Hand, a Soldier of Opportunity.

Lupai

For the very observant, you may notice that Lu Pai does not have a "va" between his first and last name. That is an indicator of his lower class. Tama, Mizha, Koruval, and Warren are all from noble bloodlines, descended from the leaders of the First Tribes. Pakku is from a wealthy merchant family that attached the "va" to their name to imply a higher status. Dr. Milan comes from a branch of the Ulvaima family, and maintains the honor-lflc due to his upper class bloodline.

Lu, on the other hand, is a farmer, which is what "Pai" means. Many craftsmen are simply given a first name, with the surname to indicate their background. The equivalent of "Carpenter", "Smith", and "Baker" in our world, so we'd know him as "Lu Farmer".

Lu does own a plot of land in Vilazozhu, and on occasion daydreams of retiring there, if he lives that long. Whether he could actually stand the quiet life after a long career of espionage and assassination is another question entirely.

CULTURE

This section is to highlight on some of the small cultural details found in this volume.

Zhumupuru Statue

Zhumupuru has been appropriated by many merchants as a symbol of prosperity. A common practice when starting a business is to buy a Zhumupuru statue similar to the one pictured on the right. The statues are made of copper, which will turn green as it ages. If a statues has fully oxidized, it indicates that the business is profitable and well established. The more ambitious and wealthy the owner is when starting out, the larger the statue. If the business fails, the statue is traditionally sold for scrap. However, sometimes the more unscrupulous will buy an older statue, to make it appear that their business is more successful than it actually is.

In the scene where Pakku is first introduced, a large statue can be seen near the door in the background of the Guild Master's office.

Mourning Shrine

In the train station, in front of the funeral car, there is a small mourning shrine for the Lady va Naza. Each item has an original symbolic meaning that has been adapted by Visionary lore.
Below I have described both the original and modern significance of each item.

White candles in red holders - Originally this item was to appease the West, and were snuffed out with the setting of the sun. In modern times they are said to represent the light of the soul returning to Vision.

Blue water bowl - This was to appease the East. Notes asking Waiziki for wisdom and mercy in times of grief were burned in the candle flames. The ashes were mixed into the water, which was sometimes used to anoint the next of kin responsible for the funeral rites. Although Visionary teachings now dictate that the bowl represents the blessings and benevolence of the Rainbow Goddess, Note Burning traditions remain unchanged.

Five maple dumplings on a green or wooden plate - This tradition is to appease the North, as the Great Green Bear would return the body to the earth and guide the spirit to the Canyon of Souls. The dumplings are made of a sweet-bread and covered in maple syrup, as the maple tree is sacred to Zhumupuru. The family would often eat bitter or salty foods. Now this offering is said to distract the cruel Dream Eater, so he does not consume the soul of the deceased. However, souls too heavy with sin will reek of their evil deeds and attract the dark god, no matter how many sweets sit at a shrine. In that case, Dream Eater will be unable to resist devouring the wicked soul. This tradition is also why honey is a part of funeral rites.

Itsuri Crests

The family and organization crests are presented in the order they joined the empire.

Vision blessed Naza at the White Mountain with His Virtue. The Sun Sages were the first people to acknowledge Naza's divinity. Naza returned to his original tribe, the war-like Ulvaima, to cease their petty squabbling for a grander goal: Unification. The first tribe they joined with were the prideful Momuru, through a long and bitter war. Once the desert tribes had been merged, Vision turned his gaze to the kingdom of Kizhimo.

Clever King Kizhimo, rather than risk his city's ruin, presented his daughter to Vision. The god was stunned by her beauty and claimed her as his wife. In time, she bore him a son. Despite their alliance, the King became nervous at the war-host stationed at his door. He told Vision of the tribes to the south that mocked Vision's power. Enraged, Vision led his army against them in the War of Cleansing. Although Rakapomo was conquered, it was at great cost. Naza, host to the holy Vision, was killed. King Kizhimo declared a fortress be built for Vision's heir on the White Mountain. It was their duty to make the world fit for Vision's inevitable return.

Once the city of Tamapa'O was complete, the High Sage sent his army to the north in Vision's name. They took the simple plains of Vilazozhu with ease, but the pirate nation and the first of the Pwama kingdoms proved more trouble. Eventually the leaders of both nations made a pact with the reigning High Sage and became Itsuri subjects, provided they could continue governing their lands. Through this agreement, the Council of Elders was formed, made up of Stewards representing each province. At last, the Great Pwama Wall had been reached, and the Itsuri gains stuttered to a halt. After decades of fighting on Zakalola's plains, High Sage Koruval called for peace. Eager for exotic imports and trade opportunities, the Merchant Guild, already an ancient organization, formally registered the Guild to pool political power, hoping for a seat on the Council of Elders.

1 Vision	2 Sun Sages	3 Ulvaima	4 Momuru
5 Kizhimo	6 Rakapomo	7 Tamapa'O Royal Family	8 Vilazozhu
9 Kuzopa	10 Zhumuwelo	11 Zakalola	12 Merchant Guild